The

CAT'S
PURR

The

CAT'S
PURR

written & illustrated by

ASHLEY
BRYAN

Atheneum · New York

Library of Congress Cataloging in Publication Data

Bryan, Ashley.   The cat's purr.

SUMMARY: Cat and Rat are friends, but when Rat tricks
Cat and plays a special cat drum, which only cats
may play, Cat winds up having swallowed the drum,
and that is how he got his purr.
[1. Folklore—Africa.   2. Cats—Fiction]   I. Title.
PZ8.1.B838Cat   1985   [E]   84-21534
ISBN 0-689-31086-2

Atheneum
Macmillan Publishing Company
866 Third Avenue, New York, NY 10022
Collier Macmillan Canada, Inc.

Text set by Linoprint Composition, New York City
Printed by Connecticut Printers, Bloomfield, Connecticut
Bound by Bookbinders, Jersey City, New Jersey
Typography by Mary Ahern

5 7 9 11 13 15 17 19 20 18 16 14 12 10 8 6

To a GREAT Niece
Janine Denny
a GREAT Nephew
Sidney Jackson
and a
GREAT Islesford Friend
Erin Fernald

all under 5!

Once upon a time, Cat and Rat were the best of friends. Uh-huh, uh-huh, they really were! They lived in huts right next to each other. And since Rat liked to copy Cat, their huts matched.

Cat planted a coconut palm tree by his hut. Rat planted one, too.

Cat wove a straw mat for the corner of his hut. Rat wove one, too. When Rat visited Cat, he'd sit on Cat's mat; and on visits to Rat, Cat sat on Rat's mat.

Cat made a bamboo flute and played sweet tunes.

"Let me play a tune, too," said Rat.

Cat let Rat play a tune, too: *too-de-loo, too-de-loo.*

Cat and Rat farmed their land together. They worked in the field each day and took good care of their vegetable patch. After work they headed home, each with his hoe.

"When the vegetables are ready, let's have a big feast," said Cat one day.

"A grand party with dancing and singing," said Rat, "uh-huh, uh-huh!"

They laughed and talked of the feast as they walked along singing, "Ho, for a feast and hi, for a song."

One night, Cat's old uncle visited and brought Cat a present. Cat unwrapped the package. There, inside, was a small drum, the smallest drum Cat had ever seen.

"It's a cat drum," the old uncle said, "passed down in the family. Now it's just for you."

"It's so small. Can I play it?" asked Cat.

"Oh, yes!" said Cat's uncle. "It's small, and there's a special way to play it. Don't rap it or beat it or poke it, or you won't get a good sound. Stroke it gently and listen."

Cat stroked the drum gently. The drum went: *purrum, purrum.*

"Oh, meow!" said Cat. "How soothing, how beautiful!"

"Take good care of the drum," Cat's old uncle said as he was leaving. "Remember now, don't rap it or beat it or tap it or poke it. Just stroke it gently. And don't let anyone else play it."

The next morning Rat called on Cat, as he always did, on the way to work in the fields. He tapped on Cat's hut door: *rap-a-tap tap, rap-a-tap tap.*

Purrum, purrum, purrum came the sound from inside Cat's hut. Rat had never heard such music before. He opened Cat's door and went in. There sat Cat on his bed, playing a small drum.

"Pit-tap-a-la-pat," cried Rat. "What a big, sweet sound and from such a small drum! It's so small you could swallow it whole! Squeek-eek, play it, Cat, uh-huh!"

Purrum, purrum, purrum, played Cat. *Purrum, purrum, purrum.*

Rat twirled about. He hummed and kicked up his feet to the purrum, purrum beat until Cat stopped drumming.

"Me now!" Rat cried.

"Oh no!" said Cat. "Mee-ow! This is a Cat family drum from my uncle."

"Pit-tap-a-la-pat," said Rat. "So what? I made my hut like yours, squeak, squee-eee. I played in the shade of your coconut tree; I sat on your mat, drank coconut milk, too. I played your flute, *too-de-loo, too-de-loo.*"

"That was different, Rat," Cat said. "My uncle said no one else plays this Cat drum. Anyway, this is not a time for drumming. Let's get to work in the fields."

Cat set the drum down on the bed.

"I must think of a good plan so that I can play Cat's drum," Rat thought. "I'll need time to think."

"I'm hungry," Rat said. "Squee-eek! If I'm to work in the fields, I've got to eat food first. I'll faint if I go without breakfast."

Cat cooked cornmeal mush and served Rat. Rat ate, but he couldn't keep his eyes off the drum. It still sang in his ears, *purrum, purrum.* His fingers itched to play it.

Rat ate slowly, bowl after bowl of cornmeal mush. Still not one good drum-playing plan popped into his head. He dawdled so long over the breakfast that it was tea time when he finished. His stomach was as tight as a drum.

"It's tea time," Rat said. "Squee-eek, and I'm still hungry. We'll work better after tea, Cat. Don't you agree?"

"Meow, I'm not hungry now," said Cat. "How can you still be hungry after swallowing so much mush?"

"It just wasn't enough mush, I guess," said Rat.

"Oh, meow," said Cat, and he served Rat the tea. "Now don't get sick. Remember, we have lots of work to do for our feast."

"Sick!" Rat thought. "That's it!"

Cat had given Rat the idea he needed. Now he knew just what to do.

"Pit-tap-a-la-pat," Rat cried as he pushed aside his cup and plate. "I'm full now and ready for work. Squee-eek."

"Pit-tap-a-la-po," Cat cried. "Here's your hoe. Meow, let's go!"

Rat was almost to the door when he moaned
and fell to the ground. He turned and tossed at
Cat's feet.

"Ooo-ooo," Rat groaned. "My belly's hurting me too bad. Squeak, Squee-eek."

"I knew you'd be sick," Cat said.

Cat helped Rat to his feet.

"Ah, poor Rat. Don't lie on the floor. Come, lie on my bed."

"Ooo-ooo. Thank you. Squeek-eek, ooo-ooo."

Cat put Rat to bed and spread a coverlet over him.

"Rest," said Cat. "When your belly is cool, come and help me till the fields."

"I will come, oh-ooo, when I'm well. We two do work so well together. Oh-ooo, oh-ooo!"

Though Rat wailed well, he was not ill at all, uh-uh! He stretched out on Cat's bed till his toes touched the drum. His plan was working, and he felt happy.

Cat left Rat to rest and set out for their vegetable patch. Rat waited until he was sure that Cat had reached the field. Then Rat threw off the coverlet, sat up and began to sing:

> *"Pit-tap-a-la-pat*
> *Pit-tap-a-la-ping*
> *Eat off Cat's food*
> *And don't pay a thing."*

Rat reached for Cat's drum and hugged it.

"I'd rather hug a drum than do hum-drum hoeing." Rat laughed. "Now it's my turn to play Cat's drum."

Rat had danced while Cat drummed, so he had not learned Cat's secret of how best to beat it.

Rat tapped the drum, no purrum. Rat beat the drum, no purrum. He poked it, no-no, no purrum! Instead of hugging Cat's drum now, Rat was so mad he could have pounded it. But by chance he stroked it. And there it was: *purrum, purrum, purrum.*

"Pit-tap-a-la-pat!" cried Rat. "What a thing, this drum. Rap it, tap it, beat it, poke it—no loud, sweet purrum. But when you stroke it—*purrum, purrum, purrum.*"

Far off in the field, Cat heard the sound. It was his drum—*purrum, purrum, purrum.* He dropped his hoe and ran toward his hut.

Rat saw Cat coming across the field. Quickly he replaced the drum at the foot of the bed. He stretched out and drew the coverlet up to his chin. He closed his eyes and pretended to be asleep. Cat ran into the room, shook Rat awake and shouted:

> *"Pit-tap-a-la-pat*
> *Pit-tap-a-la-pum*
> *Who's that knocking*
> *On my drum?*

"I fell asleep," said Rat. "I didn't hear a thing. Squee-eek, oh-ooo! My belly's hurting me too bad."

"You mean your belly's not cool yet, Rat?" Cat asked. "Well, lie down, but keep your eyes open."

"I will do as well as I can, Cat, even though I'm ill."

Cat set out alone to till the fields.

And Rat could hardly wait to play the drum again. When Cat was well out of sight, he sat up in bed and sang:

> "Pit-tap-a-la-pat
> Pit-tap-a-la-ping
> Eat off Cat's food
> And don't pay a thing."

Rat shook with excitement when he took up the drum. First he hugged it, then he stroked it more lightly than before. An even louder *purrum, purrum, purrum* came from the drum.

As Cat hoed a row of vegetables, he heard *purrum, purrum, purrum.* At once he dropped his hoe and headed for home.

Rat was again in bed and under the coverlet when Cat ran in. Cat shook Rat and cried:

> *"Pit-tap-a-la-pat*
> *Pit-tap-a-la-pum*
> *Who's that knocking*
> *On my drum?"*

"You make my belly ache more when you shake me up so," said Rat. "Oo-ooo, my belly's hurting me too bad. I didn't hear a thing."

"But, Rat, I tell you someone is knocking on my drum. I hear it in the field—*purrum, purrum, purrum.* Come now, help me, Rat."

"How can I?" said Rat. "I'm lying down, and my belly is hurting me."

"Stay in my bed till your belly's cool. But keep your eyes open. Find out who's knocking on my drum and tell me."

Cat left and closed the door. This time
though, Cat didn't go far along the path to the
field. He doubled back, ducked down and crept to
the side of the hut. There he climbed in through the
kitchen window and hid under the table.

When Rat thought that Cat was far out of sight, he sat right up in bed.

"What's this?" Cat asked himself. "Maybe Rat's belly is cool now."

He watched Rat from the hiding place under the table. He saw Rat take up the drum. Cat did not move. Rat began to sing:

    "I fooled Cat once"

Cat kept quiet.

       "I fooled Cat twice"

Cat blinked his eyes.

"I play Cat's drum"

Cat's ears twitched.

"Purrum, purrum, purrum."

"Drop that drum, Rat," cried Cat. "I've caught you at it. Mee-ow."

"You haven't caught me yet," cried Rat.

Rat dodged and scampered down as Cat leaped onto the bed.

So Cat jumped off the bed and trapped Rat in the corner.

All Rat saw was Cat's wide-open mouth and Cat's very sharp teeth. And that gave Rat a new idea.

As Cat flung himself at Rat, Rat plunged the
drum into Cat's open mouth and fled.

Cat fell against the bed. He gulped and swallowed. Down went the drum. To his surprise, Cat realized that instead of swallowing Rat, he had swallowed his drum.

Cat stroked his stomach to settle the drum. A muffled sound came from within: *purrum, purrum, purrum.*

Rat ran out of Cat's hut and past his own. He didn't stop to pack a thing, uh-uh! He kept on going, and he didn't look back. By the time Cat finally ran out of doors, Rat was long gone.

"That's that for our vegetable feast," Cat cried. "If I ever catch that Rat, I'll feast on him. Meow!"

Since that day, Cat carries his drum safely within. You can't fool Cat anymore with belly cool this and belly cool that. Uh-uh! Cat always knows now who's playing his drum because Cat alone chooses whom he'll let play.

If you're kind to Cat, he'll let you play his drum. Remember, though, don't tap it or beat it, don't rap it or poke it. Just stroke Cat gently, very, very gently. Uh-huh, uh-huh!

Listen now. Can you hear Cat purring—*purrum, purrum, purrum?*

That's cat's drum!

Purrum, purrum, purrum.

Parsons, Elsie Clews.
Folklore Of The Antilles, French and English, Part II.
New York: American Folklore Society, G. E. Stechert &
Company, 1936, page 293

10. WHY CAT EATS RAT (*Montserrat*)

Cat an' a rat going to have a morone (big fete), an' afa they went the
had the tea for the fust before they commence to work. Afa they have break
fast before they commence to work. Afa they finish everything the rat say
"Oh mon, my belly's hurting me! I can not work." And the cat says to the rat
"Go in there and lay down on my bed until your belly's cool." And after th
rat went in, it lay down on the bed an' it look up an' see a little drum on th
bed. An' after he saw the little drum on the bed he take de drum an he knock

Dink-a-ding-ding
Dink-a-ding-ding
Eat off the food
And won't pay for it.

De cat come in an' says, "Who is that knockin' my little tam'ourine? De ra
say, "I don't know. I'm layin' down. My belly hurtin' me. I don't know.
Afa de cat went out he heard de same t'ing:

Dink-a-ding-ding
Dink-a-ding-ding
Eat off the food
And won't pay for it.

De cat come in an' he ask de rat who knockin' de tam'ourine again? De ra
say, "I don't know. I'm laying down. My belly hurtin' me. I don't know.
can't attend to dat." An' de cat went out en' he stay under de table. He did no
work any more. An' after he was dere he heard the same t'ing:

Dink-a-ding-ding
Dink-a-ding-ding
Eat off the food
And won't pay for it.

An' he get up an' he went in to de rat an' he see rat playin' de drum an' singin
de song. An' he take rat an' eat 'tup. An' dat's de reason why cats eats rats

Recorded by Arthur H. Fauset